MW00880494

Wrong Bus

A STORYQUEST BOOK BY

BECCI MURRAY

For Jessie

STORYQUEST
CHOOSE THE PAGE - UNLOCK THE ADVENTURE

Copyright © Becci Murray 2020
All rights reserved. No part of this book may be reproduced or used
in any manner without written permission of the copyright owner
except for the use of quotations in a book review.

ISBN: 978-1-9162069-8-4

Published by Llama House Children's Books

Welcome to your StoryQuest challenge, the book where YOU are in charge of what happens and YOU are the star of the adventure.

Start your quest on the first page, where your challenge will be explained. At the end of each chapter you'll find two options – choose a page to decide what you want to do next.

As a bonus feature, every StoryQuest book has a SPECIAL CHARACTER hidden amongst the pages. Find the character, and they'll give you a STORYQUEST STAR. This will help you unlock the ultimate ending to your adventure.

There are SO many different paths and SO many different endings – some are good, some are bad, some are happy, some are sad. Which will you choose? Will you complete the challenge? And where will your story end?

Good luck, intrepid StoryQuester, and happy reading!

Waiting for a bus is more boring than anything else in the whole, entire universe.

Your mum's rabbiting on about something she saw on the telly (yawn), there's a man in a suit reading a newspaper (double-yawn) and old Mrs Pollychamp from next door is fiddling with her false teeth (triple-yawn), when suddenly the sky opens up and an enormous red bus bursts through the clouds.

VROOSH!

Four bright lights beam down from the bus's wheels as it lands on the road in front of you. With a hiss, the doors open and a robot walks out. She has legs like drainpipes, arms like springs and a face like a wok.

"Greetings, humanoids," she bleeps. "I am a Bio-Robotic Intelligent Android Navigator from Space Zone 12, but you can call me BRIAN."

"Hello, BRIAN," you reply, as your mum's face turns grey. "What brings you to planet Earth?"

"I am the driver of this intergalactic school bus, but my spacecraft has been hit by a meteor and my memory box has been damaged." The robot points to a dent in her forehead. "I have forgotten almost forty-four billion gigabytes of data."

"Oh, dear," you reply. "That looks painful. Does it

1

hurt?"

"Young humanoid," the robot replies, "that is like asking a tin of baked-beans if it has the tummy ache, but you can call me BRIAN." The robot scratches her head. "Did I already say that?"

"Yes, you did. Can you remember anything at all, BRIAN?"

"Well, I remember collecting these children from Miss Tentacle's School for Every Alien," she says, "and I remember it is my job to return each child safely back to their parents."

You look up through the windows of the bus. A group of alien children stares back at you. Some have flippers, some are covered in hair, some have mouths like bananas and some are asleep in the luggage rack.

"The problem is," the robot continues, "I cannot remember where their home planets are located, so I have landed here on Earth to ask for assistance." She pauses, and then, "Young humanoid, will you fly this space-bus and navigate the deepest, darkest depths of the endless universe to save these children?"

"*Me?!*" you gasp. "But I can't fly a bus!"

"Flying a bus is easy," she says, "but navigating the cosmos can sometimes prove tricky. Which is why I have some useful items to aid your success."

The robot reaches an extendable arm back into the

bus and pulls a plastic tub from under the driver's seat. You don't know what you were hoping she'd pull out from under that seat, but a packed-lunch definitely wasn't it.

"Are those...sandwiches?" you ask.

"Affirmative," grins the robot, meaning 'yes.' "Moon cheese and starfruit chutney. My favourites. Sandwiches are essential for every outer-space journey."

She points to a silver handle on the dashboard of the bus.

"We also have this rocket boost lever. With one pull, our bus will hurtle across the universe at the speed of light."

"That sounds...terrifying," you say.

"And thirdly, you have me, BRIAN, the most advanced satellite navigation robot this side of the Lunar Peninsular." You eye the big dent in BRIAN's forehead and smile politely. "So, young humanoid, will you help a broken satnav robot return these alien children to their home planets?"

A buzz of excitement zips up your spine like a bright shooting star.

"Okay," you reply, "let's do it!"

Mum's eyes bulge like a couple of ping-pong balls as BRIAN grabs you by the jumper, lifts you onto the bus and plonks you down in the driver's seat.

"That is most excellent news," bleeps the robot. "I shall return you to your mother when our quest is complete. But remember, you must locate the *correct planets* for each group of children or we shall all be lost in space forever," and with the push of a button, your space-bus soars up through the cloudy skies of planet Earth and into the endless universe.

Your StoryQuest has begun! Turn to page 42 to start your adventure.

"I'm sorry, officer," you reply. "I didn't realise I needed a license to fly this bus."

"Don't worry," the alien replies, "if you don't have a license, you can take a test. It won't take long – in fact, there's only one question." The officer takes a pamphlet out of his pocket and opens it up. "Ah, yes, here it is: which button will activate the windscreen wipers of your space-vehicle?"

Zoinks! This is the quickest driver's test *ever!* But you didn't know the bus even *had* windscreen wipers!

"If you press the correct button," the officer goes on, "I'll give you your license. But press the wrong button, and your bus will be confiscated and you'll have to catch the next space-train out of here."

There are only two buttons to choose from. One is orange and the other is pink. Which button will you press?

To press the orange button, turn to page 86.
To press the pink button, turn to page 33.

"BRIAN might be a bit dented," you tell the man in the dressing gown, "and she's forgotten forty-four billion gigabytes of data, but she's my friend and she's helping me finish this quest. I don't want to swap her."

The golden android sniffs and an oily tear runs down his face.

"Do you see that, Master Jake?" he chokes. "*That* is true loyalty. You could learn a thing or two from this young human."

"Hm," says the man in the dressing gown, "but tell me, kid, if your satnav robot's broken, how are you navigating your way through space?"

"I'm just guessing really," you tell him, "and sometimes I ask people for directions. Hey, I don't suppose you know where Sweatiolis is, do you?"

"Kid," he replies, "I've been flying this ship since 1977 – of course I know the way to Sweatiolis. All you have to do is head for the Triangular Sun and it'll be right there in front of you. I went there once with my father. Strange man. Kind of grumpy."

You thank Master Jake for his help, then the green alien shows you back to your bus and you take to the skies once again.

In the near-distance, a Triangular Sun twinkles

like a sparkly wedge of cheese. The air on the bus grows hotter as you travel towards it and you feel like a piece of corn in a microwave, about to go pop at any moment, when suddenly you notice a slivery planet orbiting the sun's highest point. It's Sweatiolis – cosmic!

Sweatiolis has fifteen yellow moons and a small space-rock hovering close to your bus. An old alien is sat on a deckchair, holding a big, red button. Her bottom is as wide as the rock and she looks like a giant potato, only more knobbly and without the mud.

"Who's that?" you whisper to BRIAN.

"She looks like a toll collector," the robot explains. "Sweatiolis has a silver forcefield protecting it. That alien will not open the barrier unless we pay her a fee."

As BRIAN searches her disc-drive for loose change, you pull up next to the rock and open the window. The toll collector grimaces through the gap as she holds out her hand. You don't have any money and it doesn't look like BRIAN does either. What are you going to do?

I'll give her a sandwich from the lunchbox. Turn to page 71.

I'll talk nicely to her and explain what's happened. Turn to page 17.

Turning the bus with lightning speed, you slam your foot on the accelerator.

VROOSH!

Your spacecraft zooms away from the avalanche and along the pear-slice road, where a mango-car suddenly pulls out of a side-street. At the last moment, you stamp on the brake and screech to a halt, where you turn to see the enormous grapes moving closer by the second.

You watch as they tumble down Kiwi Mountain, past the Banana Forest and along the pear-slice road, until one by one they slam into the side of your bus.

SPLAT! SPLAT! SPLAT! SPLAT! SPLAT! SPLAT!

The fruits explode like purple pimples, burying your bus in a sticky mess. It'll take forever to dig your way out of here.

"Perhaps we should call Miss Tentacle," suggests BRIAN. "She has family here on Fruitopia who may help us out of our sticky situation."

Hurriedly, you press the hologramophone button. Miss Tentacle appears in the aisle of the bus. She's making a noise like a sheep playing a harmonica.

"MAA-AA-AA-AA-AA-AA-AA-AA—"

When she realises you can see (and hear) her, she

stops.

"Oh, hello," she says. "I was just practising my operatic scales."

Crikey, she was *singing!*

You thought someone had stood on her tentacle.

When you explain what happened, Miss Tentacle looks out of the window. She sees the alien driver get out of his mango-car. He has four purple tentacles, a long trunk and a candyfloss beard. In a funny sort of way, he looks like an upside-down version of the headmistress.

"Well, bless my stars and moons!" Miss Tentacle exclaims. "It's my twin brother, *Mr* Tentacle. You've saved him from a grape avalanche, you wonderful human! I'll get him to call a few friends and dig you out of that mess. Keep up the good work though – you're doing a great job. Now, where did I put my tuning fork…?"

Before long, a hundred Fruitopians are digging you out of the goo and waving you off as you leave the planet Fruitopia. The blackhole is still swirling like an astronomical washing machine as you pass by, so you steer carefully around it as BRIAN pushes the satnav button on her arm.

"The fourth bus-stop we must find is on a planet called Noctron," says the robot. "To locate the planet

Noctron, we must bear left – *BLEEP!* Bear left – *BLEEP!* Bear left – *BLEEP!* Bear left – *BLEEP!*"

That's strange. This is the first time BRIAN has only given you one direction to follow, but turning left will send you into the blackhole.

"I'm not sure that's a good idea," you tell her. "Perhaps we should bear right instead."

"No!" cries the robot. "Bear left! Bear left!" She points into the blackhole. "Young humanoid, there is a *bear* on our left!"

Confused, you look out of the window. Well, blow me down with a solar wind, there really *is* a bear on your left! It's a huge bear made completely of stars, running through space like it's out for a stroll in the park.

The bear beckons you into the blackhole with his twinkly paw. Do you want to follow him?

A space-bear? Cool! Let's follow him! Turn to page 46.
A space-bear? Eek! Let's get out of here! Turn to page 25.

You activate the inflatable tyre mechanism and the wheels of your bus swell-up like four huge rubber-rings. They push against the windows like mutant slugs as the air inside them lifts your spacecraft slowly up to the surface of the ocean.

The bus bobs on the shimmering waves as you open the doors with a hiss. Five silvery children dive into the water, as their parents' heads break the surface.

You've taken the first group of children back to their home planet!

"Excellent work, young humanoid," congratulates BRIAN. "Shall we now move on to our next planet?" She presses the satnav button on her arm. "The second bus-stop we must find is on a planet called Sweatiolis. To locate the planet Sweatiolis, we must travel towards the Triangular Sun – *BLEEP!* We must chase the shooting star - *BLEEP!* Travel towards the Triangular Sun - *BLEEP!* Chase the shooting star – *BLEEP!*"

I'll travel towards the Triangular Sun please. Turn to page 55.

I'd like to follow the shooting star. Turn to page 40.

11

You carry on in the hope you have enough fuel, but your spacecraft sounds more like a steam train than a bus.

CHUG...CHUG...CHUG...CHUG...

It's jumping from star to star like a kangaroo on a pogo-stick, stuttering over planets and spluttering past moons, until suddenly, with one final cough, the engine stops.

You've run out of fuel. Your space-bus has broken down and you're floating around in the nothingness with no power. Even the hologramophone won't work, so you wait patiently until Miss Tentacle notices your lateness and sends a tow-ship out to rescue you.

Go back to the start of the book to try again, or turn to page 26 to make a different choice.

As you fly towards the brilliant white light, you realise it's not a planet, it's a nebular star.

Nebular stars are awesome! There's so much gravity on a nebular star, it acts like a super-strength magnet. Space-junk from across the universe is sucked in and stretched out like pizza dough, until it ends up like a long strand of spaghetti.

Sadly, this also means being on a bus near a nebular star is a really bad idea. The light pulls you in at half the speed of light and stretches you out like a piece of elastic.

You can't steer a bus with noodle-arms so your quest is over. But all this talk of spaghetti has made you hungry, so you order an intergalactic food delivery and feast on spaghettified spaghetti until Miss Tentacle hears about your predicament and sends you straight back to Earth.

Go back to the start of the book to try again, or turn to page 57 to make a different choice.

13

When you open the window, a terrible stink fills the bus. It smells worse than a cabbage-eating skunk in a sewer.

"Phooey!" you cry, pinching your nose. "What's that horrible smell?"

"I believe the pong you're referring to comes from the fifteen moons of Sweatiolis," says BRIAN. "They are made out of cheese and are well-known for their astronomical whiff."

The stinky air makes your head dizzy and your vision blurred. You can't see to drive, so BRIAN presses the hologramophone button and the headmistress appears in the aisle of the bus, snoring like an elephant with a trumpet stuck up its nostril.

"ZZZZZ! ZZZZZZ! ZZZZ- Oh, erm, hello," she splutters. "I was just resting my eyes." She wasn't. She was snoring like an elephant. "How can I help you?"

"Miss Tentacle, I am afraid the young humanoid has opened a window near the fifteen moons of Sweatiolis," explains BRIAN, "and the terrible whiff of cheese has overpowered their senses."

"That's awful news," says Miss Tentacle. "We must take the young human back to an Earthean doctor as soon as possible. Wait there, BRIAN – I'll send someone out to fetch you."

A tow-ship arrives. It pulls you back to your home planet, where the doctor says you'll be fine but the smell lingers on you for weeks and everyone at school thinks you stepped in something a dog did.

Go back to the start of the book to try again, or turn to page 31 to make a different choice.

"I'm not falling for that one," you tell the impish aliens, "you're making it up. Come on, get off the bus without a donut and let's see if you really *are* arrested by the Donut Police."

You usher the banana-mouthed children through the doorway and watch as they scamper away from the bus. They're heading straight for the hatch of the Blue Moon Donut Café.

"I cannot see the Donut Police," says BRIAN, with confusion, "and I cannot see the bus-stop either. I fear those alien children have been telling us lies, young humanoid – and I believe we are on the wrong planet."

Drat those pesky aliens!

What are you going to do?

I'd like to call Miss Tentacle on the hologramophone.

Turn to page 59.

I'll tell the children to get back on the bus. Turn to page 69.

You decide to talk nicely to the toll collector and explain what happened.

"Hello," you say. "How are you?"

The alien smiles.

Actually, it could be a snarl.

Whatever it is, it looks like it hurts.

"Nrgh," growls the toll collector.

"I, erm, really like your clothes," you go on. "They're very—"

But then you realise she's a talking potato and she's not wearing any clothes. Awkward.

The toll collector pushes her hand closer towards you.

"You gotta pay," she says, "so gimme your money or *CLEAR OFF!*"

The force of her voice ruffles your hair and a drop of alien spit lands on your face.

"The thing is," you say, wiping it off with the back of your hand, "I'm on a quest to save these children, but I don't have any money. Please can you press the button and let me through without paying? Just this once?"

The toll collector curls her rubbery lips up under her nose and looks carefully into your eyes. Then she

shoves the forcefield button into her mouth and crunches it up like a boiled sweet.

CHOMP! CHOMP! CHOMP!

You take that as a 'no.'

The forcefield won't be opening any time soon, not now the button is inside the toll collector's belly, so you can't get to Sweatiolis to return the second group of children. Never mind, StoryQuester – why not go back and see if the toll collector would like a nice sandwich instead?

Go back to the start of the book to try again, or turn to page 6 to make a different choice.

The golden comet leads you to a blue planet with a rippling surface. An immense ring circles around it, glittering in the light of a small, white sun. It reminds you of Saturn, but either you're seeing things or…*that ring has teeth!*

"Young humanoid," says BRIAN, "there is a giant space-eel guarding this planet. Space-eels are very rare and very dangerous. It will make entering the atmosphere quite tricky."

Okay, StoryQuester, how will you reach the planet without being eaten by the evil space-fish?

I'll fly quickly and take the space-eel by surprise. Turn to page 74.

I'll approach the eel slowly then swerve at the last second. Turn to page 99.

As you dock into the fuel space station, a pink alien scurries over to fill up your tank.

"I should warn you," she chatters, unscrewing the cap, "putting the wrong type of fuel in a spacecraft can permanently damage the engine. You'd better hope this is your lucky day." She taps on the bonnet of your bus. "All done. I'll send the bill to Miss Tentacle. Okay, then – give it a try."

A shooting-star sweeps overhead as you press the ignition button. You close your eyes, make a wish and…

VROOSH!

The new fuel turns out to be even *better* than the old fuel – huzzah! – so you leave the fuel station and head-off in search of Miss Tentacle's School for Every Alien.

"The school is in Space Zone 12," says BRIAN, "and no bump on the head will make me forget where my own galaxy is located – this way, StoryQuester!"

The satnav robot directs you across the starry plains, past the Lunar Peninsular and onto Space Zone 12, where a deep crimson planet looms up through a misty sky. There are five moons spinning madly around it, like a Ferris wheel stuck on high-speed.

Gah! Just when you think your quest is complete, the universe throws a handful of hypersonic moons at you. This is going to take some skilful driving.

What's your final move, StoryQuester?

I'll pull the rocket boost lever. Turn to page 51.
I'll let BRIAN steer us through. Turn to page 66.

"Not to worry," smiles Miss Tentacle, "you've taken all the children back to their home planets and proved you are the best intergalactic bus driver this side of the Lunar Peninsular – and frankly, I've had enough stars to last me a lifetime anyway."

The headmistress takes out a remote control and presses one of the buttons. A small bubble-like spacecraft zooms out from behind the school building and stops in front of you.

"What's that?" you gasp.

"A space-pod," Miss Tentacle replies. "*Your* space-pod, to be precise. It's a little thank you gift for all your hard work."

Your very own spacecraft – cosmic!

BRIAN opens the hatch and signals for you to climb in.

"This space-pod has been fitted with a built-in satellite navigation system," smiles the robot, "so you will have no difficulty in finding your way back to Earth. Safe journey home, young humanoid, and many thanks for your assistance."

You wave goodbye to BRIAN and Miss Tentacle, then you take to the skies of Space Zone 12 in your new space-pod, where you travel back through the endless universe until planet Earth appears in the distance.

You land at your usual bus-stop. Your mum's still standing there, her mouth's still hanging open and her face is still grey. She hasn't moved since you left.

"Do you like my new spaceship?" you ask her. "Miss Tentacle gave it to me. Where shall we go first, Mum? Aquavon, Sweatiolis, Fruitopia, Noctron? Or we could just go to Mars, if you like," and as your mum's face turns greyer than a cloudy day on the dark side of Noctron, you realise waiting at a bus-stop isn't quite so boring after all.

Congratulations! You've completed your quest and now you're the owner of a brand-new space-pod!

If you want to find the StoryQuest Star, go back to the start of the book and try your adventure again. Or take a look in the back of this book for more choose-the-page StoryQuest adventures.

You order a donut for each of the five blackcurrant-eyed aliens and before BRIAN can find her wallet to pay for them, the alien children munch them down in one bite.

CHOMP!

"Hey!" you cry. "You said the Donut Police would arrest you for going outside without a donut, so why have you eaten them?"

The aliens giggle. They've told you a lie. They don't live on this planet. They're from a place called Fruitopia and feeding donuts to a Fruitopian is like giving candyfloss to a rabbit. The sugary food stirs up their tummies like soup in a blender until —

"BLARRRRRGH!"

They're sick all over the back seat of the bus.

You'll have to take them to space-hospital for a nice dose of prune juice to sooth their grumbly tummies, so you can't carry on with your quest. But don't worry, StoryQuester, you can try again once you've cleaned up the mess.

Go back to the start of the book to try again, or turn to page 50 to make a different choice.

Blackholes are even scarier than space-eels, so there's no way you're following that bear. You watch as the starry bear vanishes into the swirling darkness and wonder what will become of the poor creature.

BRIAN presses the satnav button on her arm.

"Our final bus-stop," she repeats, "can be found on the planet Noctron. To locate the planet Noctron, we must travel towards the purple nebular – *BLEEP!* We should chase the flaming meteor – *BLEEP!* Travel towards the purple nebular – *BLEEP!* Chase the flaming meteor – *BLEEP!*"

The purple nebular is beautiful – let's go there. Turn to page 57.

The flaming meteor looks more exciting – let's chase it. Turn to page 54.

ZZZ-POP!

Miss Tentacle is taking a selfie as she appears in the aisle of the bus. When she realises you can see her, she stops pouting and holds out her phone to show you the photograph.

"Does my trunk look big in this?" she asks.

It does.

Her trunk would look big on a mammoth.

"Erm, no," you answer, "not at all, Miss Tentacle. Sorry to disturb you, but we've landed on the light side of Noctron and the children won't wake up. I'm worried they might be ill."

"They're not ill," replies the headmistress, "they're nocturnal. The Noctrons live on the dark side of their planet – they won't wake up in broad daylight. They wear sunglasses to stay awake at school, so whatever you do, don't let them go outside in the daylight or they'll go to sleep for a week."

The headmistress pauses to admire herself on the screen of her phone, and then, "By the way," she adds, "congratulations on finding your last planet. Return the bus to my school once you've located the bus-stop on the dark side of Noctron and your quest will be over. Now, where did I put my selfie-stick...?" and with a faint crackle, the hologram fades.

With no time to lose, you steer your spacecraft into the thick blackness of the dark side, where the children of Noctron stir in their sleep. A hologram of a bus flickers and a group of bat-like parents wave as their nocturnal children fly into the night.

Do you know what this means, StoryQuester? It means you've taken *all* of the children safely back to their home planets and are officially the most spectacular space navigator in the history of the cosmos!

All you have to do now is take the bus back to —

BEEP! BEEP! BEEP! BEEP! BEEP!

Take the bus back to Miss Tentacle and your quest will be —

BEEP! BEEP! BEEP! BEEP! BEEP!

And your quest will be —

BEEP! BEEP! BEEP! BEEP! BEEP!

Your quest will —

BEEP! BEEP! BEEP! BEEP! BEEP!

What in Jupiter's name is that awful beeping noise?

A red light illuminates on the dashboard. Your fuel tank is almost empty and you might not have enough power to fly back to Miss Tentacle's School for Every Alien without filling-up.

"There is a space fuel station not far from here,"

notes BRIAN, with a press of her satnav button. "But it sells a different type of fuel to the one we use in this bus. There is a chance it will work. But there is also a chance the new fuel will cause our bus to evaporate into a gazzilion tiny droplets of molten metal."

Blimey.

Well, this is quite a pickle. Will you risk filling-up with the new fuel, or see if you can make it back to school without it?

I'll carry on without filling up. Turn to page 12.

I'd like to go to the fuel station please. Turn to page 20.

Dodging the shooty-beam-beams is harder than you thought. Whoever's firing them is really good at it. They're hitting your bus with every shot.

But here's the thing about shooty-beam-beams. All they are is little green lights that go *PYOW-PYOW-PYOW!* They can't hurt you, so you steer your bus safely away from the gigantic spaceship until it's nothing more than a tiny speck of grey in the distance.

Marvellous!

"It looks like the shooting star we were following has gone," you say to BRIAN, searching the black sky. "But, look, there's the Triangular Sun. Perhaps we could go that way instead."

"A most excellent idea," the robot replies. "The Triangular Sun is a very interesting phenomenon, young humanoid. All of the sun's heat is funnelled out of its topmost tip, making it the hottest place in the entire cosmos."

Orbiting the tip of the Triangular Sun is a silvery planet surrounded by fifteen yellow moons. When you fly towards it, you come to a small floating space-rock. It's no bigger than a boulder and there's an old alien sat on it in a deckchair. She looks like a potato, she's holding a big red button and she's wearing a badge that says, Welcome to Sweatiolis.

You've found your next planet – cosmic!

"Who's that?" you ask BRIAN.

"She is a toll collector," the robot replies. "Sweatiolis has a silver-forcefield around it to keep out any unwanted visitors. That alien will not open the barrier unless we pay her a fee of 10 space dollars each."

As BRIAN checks her disc-drives for spare change, you pull up next to the rock and open the doors. The toll collector grimaces through the doorway, then she holds her hand out for your payment.

You don't have any money and it looks like BRIAN has forgotten where she put her wallet. How will you get past the potatoey alien?

I'll give her a sandwich from BRIAN's lunchbox instead of the cash. Turn to page 71.

I'll talk nicely to the toll collector and explain what's happened – she might let us through without paying. Turn to page 101.

Thinking fast, you pull the lunchbox out from under your seat and offer the toll collector a sandwich. The potatoey woman squints at it through narrowed eyes.

"Is that a sandwich?" she frowns.

"Of course it is not a sandwich," says BRIAN. "It is a cake."

That's strange. Why is your satnav robot lying about a sandwich?

"In that case," says the toll collector, "I suppose I could manage one little bite. You'll still have to pay a fee though – nobody goes through the forcefield without paying a fee."

The alien's mouth starts to salivate. Then she helps herself to one of the sandwiches, takes a bite and…

POOF!

…vanishes in a flash of blinding light.

You stare in horror at the empty deckchair.

"What did we do to her?!" you cry. "Where did she go?! And why did you tell her that sandwich was a cake?!"

"If the toll collector had known it was a sandwich, young humanoid, she would not have eaten it," replies BRIAN. "Sandwiches have special teleportation

31

powers in space – that tasty snack has transported the toll collector to the other side of this galaxy, where she can no longer charge us a fee to land on this planet."

Awesome!

Something red catches your eye from the seat of the toll collector's deckchair – it's the forcefield button! You reach out, take hold of the object and press. The silvery exterior of the planet opens up like an elevator door as the forcefield unlocks.

Double awesome!

But as Sweatiolis emerges from beneath it like a big, rusty ball-bearing, the heat of the Triangular Sun becomes almost unbearable. You'll have to cool down the air inside the bus if you want to land, otherwise you'll be roasted to a crisp.

Triple awe—

No, wait. That's not awesome at all.

What are you going to do?

To turn on the air-conditioning, turn to page 91.

To open the windows and create a breeze, turn to page 14.

You press the pink button and…
KA-BOOF!
…you activate the ejector seat.
Oops.

In the blink of an eye, a hatch in the roof opens up as the driver's chair hurls you out of the bus, where you drift through space like a stringless balloon, unsure whether you're falling *down* or floating *up*, until you enter the atmosphere of a nearby planet.

At this point, there's no question about which direction you're travelling – you're definitely falling down. But luckily the ground on this planet is soft, so it's a bit like landing on a giant marshmallow. What's more, the creatures who live here are kind aliens who love nothing more than making friends with creatures from other planets. They smother you with big, slobbery, alien kisses and accept you into their world as one of their own, where you live for three years until being discovered by a passing astronaut.

Go back to the start of the book to try again, or turn to page 5 to make a different choice.

33

You carry on, hoping you have enough fuel to reach Miss Tentacle's school, but your spacecraft sounds more like a steam-train than a bus.

CHUG, CHUG, CHUG, CHUG, CHUG...

What's more, it's jumping from star to star like a kangaroo on a pogo-stick, hopping over planets and leaping past comets, until suddenly, with one final splutter, the engine stops.

CH-CH-CH-CH-CH...CHUG.

You've ran out of fuel. Your space-bus has broken down in the middle of space and you're floating around in the nothingness with no power whatsoever. Even the hologramophone won't work without fuel, so you're forced to sit patiently until Miss Tentacle notices your lateness and sends out a tow-ship to find you.

Go back to the start of the book to try again, or turn to page 93 to make a different choice.

You've been wanting to try the rocket booster for *ages*, so you carefully take hold of the lever and pull.

Nothing happens.

"Why aren't we moving?" you ask BRIAN.

"Our exhaust pipe is blocked," the robot replies, as your bus starts shaking like a jelly on a train. "Those naughty young aliens have put something in there and the rocket booster is building up inside our engine. It will come out eventually, young humanoid, but the boost may be much bigger than we—"

KABOOM!

The size of the blast takes you by surprise. Your hands slip from the steering wheel as the bus rockets forwards. It crashes into the side of Kiwi Mountain with a loud splat, dislodging a bunch of oversized grapes that were balanced on top of its peak like purple boulders. The giant fruits thunder downhill towards your bus. Grape avalanche! Argh! Quick, get out of the way!

I'm facing the wrong direction – let's turn this bus around! Turn to page 8.

There's no time for that – I'll reverse us all out of here! Turn to page 37.

On the light side of the planet, there's a sign saying:

Welcome to Noctron

You've reached your final destination – cosmic!

The planet Noctron looks similar to Earth, but there are no buildings, no streets and no signs of life. There certainly aren't any bus-stops.

What's more, the children who live here are still asleep in the luggage rack. They've been snoring the whole journey. Do you think they're okay?

I think they're fine. Let's wake them up and tell them they're home. Turn to page 62.

I'll check with Miss Tentacle. Turn to page 26.

You put the bus into reverse, stamp your foot on the pedal and…

VROOSH!

Your spacecraft rushes backwards, away from Kiwi Mountain, away from the grape avalanche and onto the pear-slice road.

But it's hard to see where you're going when you're travelling in reverse and suddenly…

BOOF!

Your bus ploughs into a mango-car and you come to a standstill in the middle of the road. A fountain of fruit juice squirts out from the car's bonnet. The driver looks angry. In fact, he looks furious. He gets out, shakes a tentacle at you, then starts pummelling your spacecraft with pomegranate pips as the grape avalanche continues to roll down the pear-slice road.

One by one the enormous fruits slam into the side of your bus.

SPLAT!

SPLAT!

SPLAT!

SPLAT!

They explode like big, purple pimples, burying your spacecraft in a sticky mess. It'll take forever to dig your way out of here.

"We should call Miss Tentacle," suggests BRIAN. "She has family here on Fruitopia who may help us out of our sticky situation."

When you press the hologramophone button. Miss Tentacle appears in the aisle of the bus. She's making a noise like a goat with a broken trumpet.

"*MAA-AA-AA-AA-AA-AA-AA-AA*—"

Realising you can see (and hear) her, she stops.

"Oh, hello," she says. "I was just practising my operatic scales."

Crikey, she was *singing!*

You thought she'd caught her trunk in a car-door.

Hurriedly, you explain what happened and Miss Tentacle looks out of the window. She sees the alien driver throwing pomegranate seeds at your bus. He has four purple tentacles, a long trunk and a candyfloss beard. In a funny sort of way, he looks like an upside-down version of Miss Tentacle.

"That's my brother!" cries the headmistress. "That's *Mr* Tentacle!"

She glowers at you through her moon-shaped spectacles.

"Humanoid," she snarls, "I'm sending a tow-ship to pull you out of there, then you'd better start saving your pocket money – you owe my brother a new mango-car," and as the hologram flickers out, your StoryQuest comes to a very sticky end.

Go back to the start of the book to try again, or turn to page 35 to make a different choice.

The shooting star slides across the darkness like a lone firework, its golden tail glittering in the murky sky.

Quietly, you close your eyes and make a wish.

"I wish for the most epic space adventure the universe has ever known," you whisper.

As the words leave your lips, a disc-shaped spaceship swoops in from behind a distant moon. It's at least a thousand times bigger than your own spacecraft and it looks like a huge dinner plate (only fancier and with more lights).

A large window looks into the cockpit. You see a golden android sitting next to a yeti and a woman with two currant buns stuck to the sides of her head. A man in a dressing gown stands up. He sees your bus, pulls out a giant glow-stick and waves it around like a sword.

Could this be the start of the most epic space adventure the universe has ever known?

Suddenly, and without warning, a string of green lights sprays out of the spaceship like confetti.

PYOW! PYOW! PYOW! PYOW! PYOW!

"Young humanoid, the spaceship is attacking us with its shooty-beam-beams," says BRIAN. "We must do something before our bus is blasted to smithereens."

Quick, StoryQuester, do something and fast!

The shooty-beam-beams look harmless – let's land on the spaceship and say hello. Turn to page 63.
The shooty-beam-beams look dangerous – let's dodge them and get the heck out of here. Turn to page 29.

You soar through the dazzling starlit sky in your space-bus, circling planets and speeding past moons as if carried along on the wings of butterflies (really strong butterflies with big muscles), when suddenly…

ZZZ-POP!

A purple alien materialises next to you.

Yikes! Where did *she* come from?

The alien has six tentacles, pink candyfloss hair and a pair of moon-shaped spectacles perched on the end of her trunk. She peers over her glasses to inspect you like a hair she just found in her sandwich.

"BRIAN," she croaks, her voice sounding a bit like a creaky door, "why is there a *human* driving my space-bus?"

"Greetings, Miss Tentacle," the robot replies. Crikey, it's the headmistress of Miss Tentacle's School for Every Alien! "My memory was damaged in a meteor crash, so this young humanoid is taking the children back to their home planets."

The headmistress sniffs at you with her long, holographic trunk and her face flickers.

"Hmm," she breathes, "I suppose your enthusiasm is to be admired. Very well, human, I will trust you to look after these children and am most grateful for your help."

"You're welcome, Miss Tentacle," you reply.

"If you need my assistance," the headmistress goes on, "you may call me on the hologramophone. I'll help if I can, but if I have to send out a tow-ship to rescue you, your quest will be over. Now, if you'll excuse me, I have a very busy day ahead," and with a crackle, the headmistress is gone.

BRIAN presses the satnav button at the top of her arm – your journey is about to begin!

"The first bus-stop we must find is on a planet called Aquavon," says the robot. Her satnav voice sounds like the woman who reads the news on TV. "To locate the planet Aquavon we must head for the giant star-cluster – *BLEEP!* We should follow the golden comet – *BLEEP!* Head for the giant star-cluster – *BLEEP!* Follow the golden comet – *BLEEP!*"

BRIAN is the most advanced satnav robot this side of Space Zone 12, but she also has a big dent in her forehead. Your robot's not sure which way you should travel. Which one of her instructions will you follow?

To head for the giant star-cluster, turn to page 95.

To follow the golden comet, turn to page 19.

A stream of stars disappears into the swirling darkness of the blackhole as you fly towards it. The hole pulls at your spacecraft, trying to suck you into its murky depths like a fly down a plughole, but you keep your distance and eventually pass by unharmed.

Beyond the blackhole, there's an orange. That's right – an orange. An *actual* orange, only the size of a planet. There's even an apple-moon orbiting its stem.

With no toll collectors or space-eels blocking your path, you enter the planet's atmosphere and find yourself in a world made entirely of fruit.

It's quite a sight and it smells delicious. The trees have bananas for trunks, the houses are made out of coconuts, the mountains are kiwis and the pavements are lined with slices of pear. And there, next to the cherry-juice river, is a holographic bus-stop.

You've found the planet Fruitopia – cosmic!

With a squelch, you land on the sticky ground. The five alien children with furry green skin bounce to the front of the bus. They jump through the open doorway, run past their parents and disappear around the back of the bus.

"Okay, BRIAN," you say, "only one planet left – let's get on with our quest."

You press the ignition button to start the engine. *CHUG, CHUG, CHUG, CHUG…*

But the bus won't start.

"The children of Fruitopia are well-known for making mischief," says BRIAN. "I fear they have played a trick on us by somehow disabling our spacecraft."

Oo, the little scallywags!

What will you do, StoryQuester?

I'll get out and see if I can fix it. Turn to page 76.

Let's pull the rocket booster lever – that should get the engine started. Turn to page 35.

Being inside a blackhole is strangely unreal. Your bus drifts through an obstacle course of curious objects (a hat stand, a cement mixer, an old cruise ship, a piano, even the Statue of Liberty), all bent out of shape by the pull of the blackhole. And amongst the chaos, a big sparkly bear waves hello as he surfs through the swirling darkness on the back of an old ironing-board.

Suddenly, a starry man leaps out from behind a giant food-blender.

"Aha!" he shouts. "At last, I have you, bear! Prepare to meet thy doom as I thwart you with my mighty sword!"

The man swings a starry weapon and the bear freezes. The poor creature looks terrified.

"Excuse me," you call out of your window, "has that bear done something wrong? Only, I think you're frightening him."

The man turns his gigantic head to peer through the windscreen of your spacecraft. His eyeball alone is the size of your bus. It's as if a whole galaxy is alive in his face.

"Listen, oh small and insignificant human," says the man, "two thousand years ago, that bear stole my belt. And what's the good of a famous huntsman if his trousers keep falling down?"

"You're a famous huntsman?" you frown.

The man pulls a face like you just passed wind.

"Yes," he says. "Don't you recognise me? I'm the mighty Orion, hero of Greek mythology, son of Poseidon, eternal hunter of the skies. You must've seen me in a film or something?"

"I don't think so," you reply, "and I don't want to upset you, but I'm not sure you *are* the son of Poseidon – I think you're a constellation."

"*HOW DARE YOU INSULT THE MIGHTY ORION?!*" The universe shudders at the sound of Orion's voice, and then, "What's a constellation?" he adds.

"It's a pattern of stars," you explain. "Sometimes the stars make up the shape of an animal, or an object, or, well, a huntsman."

Orion looks himself up and down.

"In that case, you might be right." He shrugs. "But I'm still going to thwart this bear with my mighty sword."

The petrified animal cowers behind a passing marshmallow, his paws in front of his eyes. You can't let the huntsman thwart the poor creature, even if he *has* stolen his belt.

"Please don't hurt him," you say. "If he's taken

something of yours, why don't you just ask for it back?"

Orion thinks about this for a moment.

"Eternal huntsmen don't *ask* for things," he says, "they thwart people with their mighty swords. That's how the universe works – it's how the universe has *always* worked."

"But, Orion, you *are* the universe," you tell him. "Or part of it, at least. So why not make a change, break the mould, be the exception?"

The starry man frowns at your wise words.

"Well, I suppose I could give it a try," he replies. Orion looks at the terrified creature. "Hey, you, insignificant bear, please can I have my belt back?"

Timidly, the animal comes out from behind his marshmallow and takes off the belt.

"I didn't mean to upset you, Orion," he says, holding out the row of twinkling stars. "I thought we were playing a game. You can have your belt back, but first…I think the human needs *this.*"

Taking the middle star from Orion's belt, the great bear places it into your hand. There's a picture of Miss Tentacle on one side and the number 78 on the other.

"A StoryQuest Star!" you cheer. "Wow, thank you. But I can't accept this – it belongs to Orion."

"Oh, don't worry about it," says the huntsman. He

fastens what's left of his belt around his waist. "As long as my trousers stop falling down, I'm happy. Just memorise the number then give the star to Miss Tentacle when you finish your quest to unlock the ultimate end to your story. Now get out of here, irrelevant mortal – a blackhole is no place for a human."

With that, Orion takes hold of the bus and hurls you out of the blackhole, where your spacecraft follows the path of a smouldering meteor through the starlit skies of the endless universe.

Congratulations, you've found the StoryQuest star!
Turn to page 54 to continue your quest.

"Excuse me," you call into the back of the bus, "do any of you live here, or have we landed on the wrong planet?"

One of the children stands up. She's green and hairy like a kiwi fruit, her mouth is bent up like a banana and her eyes are like two purple blackcurrants. What's more, you're fairly sure her legs are made out of rhubarb.

"Yes, we live here," she replies, nudging the identical aliens on either side of her. "But you have to buy us all donuts before we get off the bus – it's the law here. If we're caught outside without a donut, we'll be arrested by the Donut Police. Isn't that right, everyone?"

The other green aliens nod keenly.

BRIAN doesn't remember buying the aliens donuts before, but there are lots of things BRIAN doesn't remember. Do you want to buy them donuts, or tell them to get off the bus without any sugary treats?

I'd like to buy them all donuts. Turn to page 24.
Nope, they're not having any donuts. Turn to page 16.

You pull the rocket boost lever and your space-bus blasts forwards at the speed of light.

VROOSH!

You're pinned to the back of your seat as if stuck there with glue and BRIAN slides down the aisle like a bowling ball, hitting the back seat in a clatter of arms and legs.

"Are you hurt?" you call out, as the bus speeds on.

"That is like asking a dustbin lid if it has the toothache," replies the robot. "Please concentrate on steering the bus, young humanoid – the five moons will be difficult to navigate."

With a pull of the steering wheel, the nose of your spacecraft lifts and the bus hops over the first moon.

VROOSH!

You slam your foot on the accelerator and your spacecraft moves faster still. You miss the second moon by the skin of your tyres, as the next two swerve in at you from opposite directions.

VROOSH!

You steer left.

VROOSH!

You steer right.

VROOSH!

And your bus slides neatly between the two moons as your rocket boost comes to an end.

Suddenly, the fifth and final orb looms up from below the bus. It's huge, it's pink and it's right in your path, so you close your eyes and brace yourself for the impact, as the moon slams into your spacecraft.

GLOB-OB-OB-OB-OB!

But, wait a minute. That's not the sound of a moon crashing into a bus. That's the sound of a *trifle* crashing into a bus. And strangely, when you open your eyes, the world outside has turned pink and wobbly.

"W-where are we?" you stutter.

BRIAN picks herself up off the floor and moves to the front of the bus.

"The fifth moon appears to be made out of strawberry jelly," notes the robot. "It is not unusual for moons to be made out of edible substances, young humanoid. Cheese is the most common, but jelly is quite popular too. I believe the other moons of this planet are made out of bubble-gum."

Yum!

The weight of your bus is too heavy for the jelly-moon to hold up, so you're not stuck inside it for long. You slide through the gooey orb like a pebble through quicksand, moving down towards the bottom of the moon until finally slipping free with a very wobbly...

PWUCK-K-K-K-K!

Below, you see a holographic sign saying:

Miss Tentacle's School for Every Alien

A purple alien with pink candyfloss hair comes out of a metal building as you land on the dusty ground and climb out of the bus.

"Welcome to my school," smiles Miss Tentacle, "and congratulations on completing your quest – you are officially the best space navigator in the universe. Now, tell me, human, do you have the StoryQuest Star?"

If you have the StoryQuest Star, turn to the page number you saw twinkling on it when Orion handed it over.
If you don't have the star, don't worry – you're still an awesome StoryQuester! Turn to page 22.

Putting the space-bus in gear, you whizz after the flaming meteor. Smoke billows out from its hot surface, making your pathway difficult to navigate, but when the air clears a beautiful planet appears through the smog.

The planet looks a lot like Earth. It has green land, blue oceans and purple mountains, with wispy white clouds hanging over it like cobwebs. One side of the globe is lit by three sparkling suns, while the other lies in complete darkness.

Where would you like to land?

To land on the light side of the planet, turn to page 36.
To land on the dark side of the planet, turn to page 93.

The Triangular Sun sparkles in the near-distance like a glittering wedge of cheese. There's a silvery planet orbiting its highest point. It has fifteen yellow moons and a small space-rock hovering nearby.

On the rock, an old alien is sat on a deckchair. Her bottom is as wide as the rock and she looks like a giant potato, only more knobbly and without the mud. She's holding a big, red button and wearing a badge that reads:

Welcome to Sweatiolis.

You've found the second planet – cosmic!

"Who's that?" you whisper to BRIAN.

"She is a toll collector," the robot explains. "Sweatiolis has a silver forcefield to protect it from unwanted visitors. The toll collector will not open the barrier unless we pay her a fee."

As BRIAN searches her disc-drive for loose change, you pull up next to the rock and open the window.

The toll collector grimaces through the gap as she holds out her hand.

You don't have any money and it doesn't look like BRIAN does either.

How are you going to get past the grumpy toll collector?

I'll give her a sandwich from the lunchbox. Turn to page 31.

I'll talk nicely to her and explain what's happened. Turn to page 105.

The nebular is a long stretch of purple dust, hanging in space like a beautiful painting. You've never seen dust so lovely before.

At the centre of the nebular, there's a brilliant white light. You're not sure what it is – it could be an incredibly bright star, or it could be a luminous planet.

Do you want to take a closer look and find out?

Yes, please, let's fly closer and take a look. Turn to page 13.

Nah, that's okay, thanks – I'll follow the meteor instead. Turn to page 54.

The space station looks like an enormous spider hanging down from an invisible thread. There are no planets nearby, so you dock into the station to ask for directions.

An alien in a red uniform approaches your vehicle. He has a neck like a giraffe, curly hair and a face that looks as if somebody stood on it. He bends down to eye you through the open window of your bus.

"Hallo, hallo, hallo," he says, "what've we got 'ere then?"

This platform isn't just a space station. It's a space *police* station – the perfect place to ask for directions.

"Hello, officer," you smile. "I'm looking for a planet called Fruitopia. Would you mind telling me how to get there?"

"No problem," the officer replies. "But first things first. Driver's license, please," and he holds out a hand.

Uh oh. You didn't know you needed a license to fly a space-bus. What will you tell him?

I'll tell him the truth. Turn to page 5.

I'll make something up so I don't get into trouble. Turn to page 89.

ZZZ-POP!

When you press the hologramophone button, Miss Tentacle appears in the aisle of the bus. She's covering up her tentacles with a towel and her candyfloss hair is as flat as a pancake. It looks like she just got out of the bath.

"Sorry to bother you," you say to the headmistress, "but I wanted to ask your advice. You see, I've dropped some of the children off at the Blue Moon Donut Café and—"

"The Blue Moon Donut Café?!" cries Miss Tentacle, almost dropping her towel. "There aren't any bus-stops by the Blue Moon Donut Café – you're on the wrong planet! You haven't given the Fruitopian children any donuts, have you?"

You watch as the children with the banana-mouths climb through the hatch of the café and start shovelling donuts into their faces.

"Erm, no, but—"

"Well, that's something at least," interrupts the headmistress. "Wait where you are and I'll send one of the teachers over to round up the children. Then it's back to Earth for you, human – we can't have you dropping children off on the wrong planets, there's too much paperwork involved. Thanks for your help though. Now, where did I put my shampoo…"

The headmistress flickers out and your StoryQuest comes to an end. Try making a different choice and watch out for those pesky Fruitopian children – they're always up to no good!

Go back to the start of the book to try again, or turn to page 16 to make a different choice.

You take hold of the rocket boost lever and pull.

VROOSH!

Your bus shoots forwards at the speed of light, pinning you to the back of your seat, so you tilt the steering wheel and the nose of the spacecraft lifts. Your bus rushes to the surface of the water and bursts out through the rolling waves like a big, rectangular dolphin, where it shoots up past the island, away from the bus-stop, through the planet's atmosphere and into the darkness of space.

Wow, that rocket booster sure has got some welly!

A bit *too* much welly perhaps.

By the time the boost ends, you're fifty-two-billion lightyears away from the planet Aquavon. It's going to take six months for you to find your way back and the children's parents will all be quite cross when you get there. Have you considered emigrating to Venus? I hear it's nice there at this time of year.

Go back to the start of the book to try again, or turn to page 80 to make a different choice.

"Wakey wakey, rise and shine!" you call into the back of the bus. "You're home now! Up you get!"

The children of Noctron yawn loudly and stretch out their wings, so you open the doors and usher them through – perhaps being outside will wake them up a bit.

But as the sunlight hits their faces, the aliens curl up on the ground, fold their wings over their heads and go back to sleep. They're snoring happily and they won't wake up no matter how loudly you shout.

You're forced to tell Miss Tentacle, who immediately calls the Noctron-parents to collect their children. Oh, shucks!

Don't worry, StoryQuester – try this part of your challenge again and your mission will soon be complete.

Go back to the start of the book to try again, or turn to page 36 to make a different choice.

You're right – the shooty-beam-beams are harmless rays of light, and there's a small docking bay on the side of the spaceship, so you fly towards it and carefully land the bus.

You're greeted by a little green man with big ears. He leads you and BRIAN to the cockpit of the spaceship, where he addresses the rest of the crew.

"Arrived those from the bus they have," says the little green alien. "Cheeky nuisances with no respect for our shooty-beam-beams they are."

"Sorry, but we didn't mean to be cheeky," you reply. "We just stopped by to say hello. You see, I'm on a quest to return a group of alien school children back to their home planets and—"

"Well, *really!*" the golden android cuts in. At the sound of his voice, the yeti groans and puts his head in his paws. "Who in their right mind sends a young human being on a *quest*? It's ludicrous, that's what it is. Master Jake, are you hearing this?"

"Yes," sighs the man in the dressing gown, "I am *always* hearing you." He looks carefully at BRIAN. "Hey, you're a Bio-Robotic Intelligent Android Navigator, aren't you?"

"I am," the robot replies, "but you can call me

BRIAN. My memory box has been damaged in a meteor crash, so this young humanoid is helping me navigate the universe and return these children to their home planets."

The man thinks for a moment.

Then he turns to ask you a question.

"Say, kid, how'd you like to swap robots?"

Before you can answer, the golden android gasps dramatically.

"Swap me for a broken Bio-Robotic Intelligent Android Navigator?!" he cries. "Master Jake, you can't possibly mean that! Why would you want to *swap* me? All I ever do is look after you all! I cook, I clean, I mop the floor, I make the beds, I iron your dressing gowns, I polish the lasers, I put your glow-sticks on charge overnight, I make a lovely light chocolate soufflé with a raspberry jus…"

The woman flying the spaceship moves the currant buns over her ears as the android goes on with his list.

"Listen, kid," the man whispers, "*your* robot's damaged, but mine's as good as new. Look at him – he's all shiny and polished and not annoying at all. And his chocolate soufflé really *is* delicious."

"…I pull the yeti hairs from the plughole, I bake buns for the princess, I go, 'pyow-pyow-pyow,' through the little microphone when we fire the shooty-beam-beams, I hide all the sharp kitchen utensils when your father visits…"

"See? You'd be crazy not to take me up on the offer," says the man. "Go on, kid – whadda you say?"

If you want to swap BRIAN for the android, turn to page 67.

If you want to keep BRIAN, turn to page 6.

When you ask BRIAN to steer your spacecraft through the five moons of Miss Tentacle's planet, the robot's eyes sparkle like jewels.

"I would *love* to drive the bus!" she beams. "Young humanoid, leave this to me."

Fasten your seat-belt, StoryQuester – you're about to find out why your satnav robot crashed this bus in the first place.

Taking the steering wheel, BRIAN places her *incredibly heavy iron foot* onto the accelerator (oh, dear) and…

THUD!

Her foot lands on the pedal like a tank falling off a cliff and the bus lurches forwards. It speeds into the path of the first moon, which pings your spacecraft across the galaxy and into the deepest, darkest realms of the outer cosmos.

You're lost in space and that's hard moon-cheese to swallow so close to the end of your quest, but don't give up now – Miss Tentacle is relying on you!

Go back to the start of the book to try again, or turn to page 20 to make a different choice.

"Okay," you reply, "I'll swap robots. But only if BRIAN's not upset about it."

"That is like asking a washing machine if it cries at sad films," remarks BRIAN, and she goes over to introduce herself to the yeti.

As you walk back to the docking bay, your shiny new android doesn't stop talking.

"Well, this is just lovely, isn't it?" he huffs. "You give people the best years of your life and what do they do? Swap you out like a library book, that's what. I've mopped these floors more times than I care to think of and I daren't even mention what I once had to clean from those toilets…"

The android goes on to tell you *exactly* what he cleaned from those toilets. He does tend to go on a bit, but at least he's not got a dent in his head.

When the android finally stops talking, you settle into the driver's seat and press the ignition button.

"Right then," you say, "which way to Sweatiolis?"

The android blinks with confusion.

"Why are you asking *me?* Doesn't this bus have a satnav robot?"

Your bus *did* have a satnav robot, but you just swapped her for a cleaning android. Which means

BRIAN is on the most epic space adventure the universe has ever known and you're stuck here with a talking vacuum cleaner.

You can't finish your quest without a satnav, StoryQuester, but Master Jake was right – the golden android really *does* make a yummy chocolate soufflé, so it's not all bad.

Nom, nom, nom!

Go back to the start of the book to try again, or turn to page 63 to make a different choice.

"Get back on the bus!" you call out to the young aliens. "We know you've been lying and we know we're on the wrong planet! If you don't come back, I'm calling Miss Tentacle to tell her what you've been up to!"

The mischievous aliens huff loudly. They crinkle their faces and narrow their little blackcurranty eyes. Then they stomp back onto the bus, sit down in their seats and fold their arms in a sulk.

The fruit-faced aliens are full of mischief and like playing tricks on people – you'd better keep an eye on them from now on.

Leaving the Blue Moon Donut Café, you decide to travel away from the giant star cluster to follow the golden comet instead. The icy orb leads you to a blue planet with a rippling surface. An immense ring circles around it, glittering in the light of a small, white sun.

It reminds you of Saturn.

But either you're seeing things or…*that ring has teeth!*

"Young humanoid," says BRIAN, "there is a giant space-eel guarding this planet. Space-eels are very rare and very dangerous. It will make entering the atmosphere quite tricky."

Okay, StoryQuester, how will you reach the planet without being eaten by the evil space-fish?

I'll fly quickly and take the space-eel by surprise. Turn to page 74.

I'll approach the eel slowly then swerve at the last second. Turn to page 97.

You pull the lunchbox out from under your seat and offer the toll collector a sandwich. The potatoey woman squints at it through narrowed eyes.

"Is that a sandwich?" she frowns.

"Of course it is not a sandwich," says BRIAN. "It is a cake."

That's strange. Why is your satnav robot lying about a sandwich?

"In that case," says the toll collector, "I suppose I could manage just one little bite. You'll still have to pay a fee though – nobody goes through the forcefield without paying a fee."

The alien's mouth starts to salivate. Then she helps herself to one of the sandwiches, takes a bite and…

POOF!

…vanishes in a flash of blinding light.

You stare in horror at the empty deckchair.

"What did we do to her?!" you cry. "Where did she go?! And why did you tell her that sandwich was a cake?!"

"If the toll collector had known it was a sandwich, young humanoid, she would not have eaten it," replies BRIAN. "Sandwiches have special teleportation powers in space – that tasty snack has transported the toll collector to the other side of this galaxy, where she can no longer charge us a fee to land on this planet."

Awesome!

Something red catches your eye from the seat of the toll collector's deckchair – it's the forcefield button! You reach out, take hold of the object and press. The silvery exterior of the planet opens up like an elevator door as the forcefield unlocks.

Double awesome!

But as Sweatiolis emerges from beneath it like a big, rusty ball-bearing, the heat of the Triangular Sun becomes almost unbearable. You'll have to cool down the air inside the bus if you want to land, otherwise you'll be roasted to a crisp.

Triple awe—

No, wait. That's not awesome at all.

What are you going to do?

To turn on the air-conditioning, turn to page 91.

To open the windows and create a breeze, turn to page 103.

"Thanks, but we don't have time for donuts," you say to the human-like alien. "I'm on a quest to take these children back to their home planets, but I can't find the bus-stop. Do you know where it is?"

"There ain't no bus-stops on the Planet of the Blue Moon," sings the man. "There ain't no bus-stops by order of the King, uh huh huh."

His left leg wiggles with a life of its own and his top lip curls up like an old sandwich. This guy is pottier than a plant pot. You're not sure he knows where his elbow is, let alone where the bus-stop is.

Will you believe the crazy donut seller and leave this planet, or ask the school children if you're in the right place?

I'll trust the donut seller, leave this planet and follow the golden comet instead. Turn to page 19.

I'd like to ask the school children if we're in the right place. Turn to page 50.

You point the bus at the eel's face and slam your foot on the accelerator.

VROOSH!

Hearing the roar of your engine, the creature turns with surprise. Giant eels are used to spaceships flying *away* from them, not *towards* them, and the bonnet of your bus is heading right for the middle of its face.

The creature's eyes bulge like gobstoppers, until suddenly, at the very last second, it ducks out of the way and you slide down its slippery back like a penny on ice.

WHEEEEEEEE!

Down and down you spiral, away from the eel's head and off the end of its tail, into the atmosphere of the glistening blue planet.

Whoa, excellent driving skills, StoryQuester!

As you swoop through the cloudy sky, you realise this planet is a giant ball of crystal-clear water. The only land is a small island with the hologram of a bus hovering over it. It's a bus-stop, and it looks like you've found your first planet.

Cosmic!

But landing a bus on that tiny little island is going

to be tricky.

Do you want to try?

Yes, please – let's do this! Turn to page 80.
No, thanks – let's not! Turn to page 90.

You've never inspected a bus before, but there doesn't seem to be anything wrong with it. At the back of the bus, there are no dents, no bits hanging off it, not even so much as a scratch, and you're about to give up when something yellow catches your eye.

Cripes! There's a bunch of bananas stuck in the exhaust pipe – so *that's* why it wouldn't start. Those pesky Fruitopian children must have put them there.

When you've unblocked the exhaust pipe and eaten a yummy banana or two, you're back in the velvety skies of the infinite universe and on your way to the final planet.

BRIAN presses the satnav button on her arm.

"The next bus-stop we must find is on a planet called Noctron," she says. "To locate the planet Noctron, we must bear left – *BLEEP!* Bear left – *BLEEP!* Bear left – *BLEEP!* Bear left – *BLEEP!*"

That's strange. This is the first time BRIAN has only given you *one* direction. And if you turn left, you'll be gobbled up by the same blackhole you were so careful to avoid earlier on.

"I'm not sure bearing left is a good idea, BRIAN," you reply. "Perhaps we could go right instead, or—"

"No!" cries the robot, her antenna buzzing. "Bear

left! Bear left! Bear left! Young humanoid, *there is a bear on our left!"*

Through the window, you see a giant bear made of stars running through space. The creature is going into the blackhole and he's beckoning you with his big sparkly paw.

Do you want to follow him?

A space-bear? Cool! Let's follow him! Turn to page 46.
A space-bear? Eek! Let's get out of here! Turn to page 25.

"You've found the StoryQuest Star!" smiles Miss Tentacle. "That's wonderful news. Now, I believe we have one last home planet to visit – come along, human, I'll fly you back to Earth in my private space-jet."

The headmistress leads you to a shiny spacecraft. It has twelve rocket boosters, a golden rudder and a little red flag on its nose. It looks like you'll be travelling home in style.

Miss Tentacle climbs into the jet as you take the seat next to her.

"Thanks for the brilliant adventure, BRIAN," you call from the window, with a wave of your hand. "I hope we meet again someday."

"I'm sure we will meet again soon," smiles the robot. "But for now, goodbye, young humanoid."

You take to the starlit skies for one last time, soaring back through the infinite universe, until planet Earth appears in the distance. Miss Tentacle lands at your usual bus-stop. Your mum's still standing there, her mouth's still hanging open and her face is still grey (and it goes a bit greyer when the betentacled headmistress follows you out of the space-jet).

Miss Tentacle tosses the StoryQuest Star into the

air like a coin, where it hangs over your head, spinning in circles, until suddenly, with a bright flash of light, it turns into the flickering hologram of a bus.

"I don't understand," you say. "Why is there an intergalactic bus-stop here on Earth?"

"It's for you," smiles the alien. "Let's call it a little thank you gift. BRIAN's memory will be fixed by tomorrow morning and *this* will be one of her stops. I'd like *you* to be the first human child to attend Miss Tentacle's School for Every Alien."

Your spine tingles with excitement.

"Cosmic!" you cry, gazing up at the glittering hologram, and as your mum's face turns greyer than a cloudy day on the dark side of Noctron, you realise waiting at a bus-stop isn't quite so boring after all.

Congratulations! You've found the ultimate end to your story and tomorrow morning you'll be the first human to attend Miss Tentacle's School for Every Alien. Wowsers! You're a StoryQuest hero!

If you'd like to read more StoryQuest adventure books, take at look in the back of this book.

As your bus swoops down towards the tiny island, you realise the target is even smaller than it first appeared. Landing a bus on it will be like trying to fit an elephant on a postage stamp.

And so, clinging tightly to the steering wheel you plummet towards the planet, where you miss the island and nosedive into the water.

SPLASH!

Your bus sinks like a boulder. The windows are closed and there's plenty of air, but the frame of your spacecraft creaks under the weight of the water as you drop towards the seabed.

An eerie light shines up through the murky shadows. There's something down there, something huge, and as the haze clears an underwater city emerges. Its buildings are lit by lilac-coloured streetlamps and pebbled roads wind in and out of the algae-covered parks.

You land in the middle of a town square. The aliens who live here stop what they're doing to gawp up at this unexpected arrival. They have silvery skin, flippers for feet and their eyes are the size of footballs.

Five children waddle to the front of the bus. They tap on the door with their flippers.

"I'm sorry," you tell them, "but I can't open the door underwater. I won't be able to breathe. We need to get back to the surface so I can let you out."

To activate the automatic tyre inflator, turn to page 11. If you'd rather use your rocket-booster, turn to page 61.

A giant space-eel is scarier than a maths teacher with an algebra test, but bravely you face the beast and slowly press the accelerator.

The eel sees you. Its eyes narrow. It licks its gelatinous lips as a wicked smile creeps over its face. A bus full of children is like a tasty tin of baked beans to a giant space-eel and he wants you all in his belly.

Nom, nom, nom!

The monster opens its huge jaws and a bus-rattling roar blasts out of its mouth.

GRAAAAAAW!

As its teeth snap closed, you swerve left, whizz past its head and enter the planet's atmosphere. You should be safe in here – the eel can't leave the realms of its outer-space home.

But suddenly, the terrible beast whips out a tongue the size of Italy and wraps it around your bus like a frog catching a fly. A gloop of space-eel spit seeps in through an open window as you're pulled away from the planet and into the eel's mouth. It drips onto your lap like an unset jelly and then…

GULP!

The world goes dark.

Luckily, your bus is too crunchy for the space-eel to chew, so it swallows you whole and no-one gets hurt. You'll pass through the creature's digestive system in two to three days, along with everything else it has eaten today, by which time the children's parents will be sick with worry.

Try taking the huge fish by surprise on your next attempt, StoryQuester, and you'll soon be on your way to Aquatron.

Go back to the start of the book to try again, or turn to page 84 to make a different choice.

"Donuts all round, please," you say to the human-like man in the diner. "But after that we really must get on with finding our first bus-stop."

"No problem, kid." He hands you a box of the sugary treats, then picks up a smaller container. "And this one's just for you."

Inside the container you find a double-layered, chocolate covered donut with rainbow sprinkles.

"For me?" you gasp. "But why?"

"There ain't no bus-stops on the Planet of the Blue Moon, kid," he whispers, "so I reckon you're on the wrong planet. But this donut sandwich should put you back in the right place. Just eat it, then follow the golden comet."

This guy is crazy. You have no idea what he's talking about, but you take the donut sandwich and thank him for the advice. As the whiff of chocolatey gooiness drifts up your nose, you lift the sandwich up to your mouth, sink your teeth in and…

POOF!

The world around you vanishes in a blinding flash of light and you find yourself back in the velvety skies of outer-space.

"W-what happened?" you gasp. "Where's the

diner gone?"

"The diner has not gone anywhere," replies BRIAN. "That donut sandwich has teleported our spacecraft to the other side of the galaxy. We seem to be back where we started, young humanoid."

Whoa, that was the best donut sandwich *ever!*

A golden comet glitters across the sky. You remember the words of the man in the diner and smile, steering your space-bus towards it.

The comet leads you to a blue planet with a rippling surface. A huge ring circles around it, sparkling in the light of a small, white sun. It reminds you of Saturn, but either you're seeing things or...*that ring has teeth!*

"Young humanoid," says BRIAN, "there is a giant space-eel guarding this planet. Space-eels are very rare and very dangerous. It will make entering the atmosphere quite tricky."

Okay, StoryQuester, how will you reach the planet without being eaten by the evil space-fish?

I'll fly quickly and take the space-eel by surprise. Turn to page 74.

I'll approach the eel slowly then swerve at the last second. Turn to page 82.

You press the orange button and…

SQUEEEEAK!

…the big windscreen wiper on the front of your bus drags painfully over the glass.

Marvellous!

"You have excellent button-choosing skills," remarks the police officer, "the best I've ever seen, in fact. I can't tell you how many people press the ejector seat button instead of the wipers. Anyway, here's your license."

He hands you a certificate with gold writing on it.

"Thank you," you say. "Can you tell us how to get to Fruitopia now please?"

"I sure can," replies the police officer, pointing towards the blackhole. "Just fly past that deadly tunnel of darkness and Fruitopia will be on your left," and with that, the officer goes back to his work.

Leaving the police station, you notice a stream of stars disappearing into the churning depths of the blackhole. It pulls at your bus as you fly towards it, but you keep your distance and somehow manage to pass by unharmed.

Phew!

Beyond the blackhole, there's an orange. That's

right – an orange. An *actual* orange, only the size of a planet. There's even an apple-moon orbiting its stem.

With no toll collectors or space-eels blocking your path, you enter the planet's atmosphere and find yourself in a world made entirely of fruit.

It's quite a sight and it smells delicious. The trees have bananas for trunks, the houses are made out of coconuts, the mountains are kiwis and the pavements are lined with slices of pear. And there, next to the cherry-juice river, is a holographic bus-stop.

You've found the planet Fruitopia – cosmic!

With a squelch, you land on the sticky ground. The five alien children with furry green skin bounce to the front of the bus. They jump through the open doorway, run past their parents then disappear around the back of the bus.

"Wow, that was easy," you smile. "Okay, BRIAN, only one planet left – onto the next bus-stop!"

You press the ignition button to fire-up the engine.

CHUG…

CHUG…

CHUG…

CHUG…

But the bus won't start.

"The children of Fruitopia are well-known for making mischief," notes BRIAN. "I fear they have played a trick on us by somehow disabling our spacecraft."

Oo, the little scallywags!

What will you do, StoryQuester?

I'll get out and see if I can fix it. Turn to page 76.

Hm, let's pull the rocket booster lever – that should do it. Turn to page 35.

You decide to make something up so you don't get into trouble.

"I can't show you my license," you say to the officer. "Because, erm, my robot ate it."

BRIAN scratches her dented head.

"Did I?" she frowns. "I do not remember that. I am terribly sorry, young humanoid. What an awful thing for me to do."

The police officer wrinkles his face to the size of a prune. Then he puts a pair of handcuffs on BRIAN's wrists.

"Eating somebody's driver's license is a very serious offence," he tells the robot. "You'll have to come into the station for questioning, I'm afraid."

Oh, no! You told a lie and now BRIAN is being taken into custody for eating your imaginary driver's license. Quick, StoryQuester, go back and make a different choice before your robot ends up behind bars!

Go back to the start of the book to try again, or turn to page 58 to make a different choice.

Instead of landing on the tiny island, you hover your bus close to the land and open the doors. The five scaly aliens who live on Aquavon waddle along the aisle, waving their flippers and chattering like dolphins, as one by one they leap out of the bus and into the water.

A shoal of parents bobs up through the waves. They smile, waving their fins in thanks, before taking their amphibious children down to their underwater home. You've taken the first group of children back to their home planet – great work, StoryQuester!

BRIAN congratulates you with a bleep of joy, then she presses the satnav button at the top of her arm.

"The second bus-stop we must find is on a planet called Sweatiolis," she says. "To locate the planet Sweatiolis we must travel towards the Triangular Sun – *BLEEP!* We should chase the shooting star - *BLEEP!* Travel towards the Triangular Sun - *BLEEP!* Chase the shooting star – *BLEEP!*" Where to next, mighty StoryQuester?

To go towards the Triangular Sun, turn to page 55.
To chase the shooting star, turn to page 40.

Your bus plunges into the thick darkness like a cherry into a trifle. Wow, it's creepy here! But the last group of children stirs in their sleep as you land with a bump on the grassy planet.

Yawning, they move down the aisle and towards the open doorway. A hologram of a bus flickers alight and a group of bat-like parents waves as their nocturnal children fly eagerly off the bus.

Do you know what this means, StoryQuester? It means you've taken *all* of the children safely back to their home planets and are officially the most spectacular space navigator in the history of the cosmos.

All you have to do now is take the bus back to—

BEEP! BEEP! BEEP! BEEP! BEEP!

Take the bus back to school and your quest will be—

BEEP! BEEP! BEEP! BEEP! BEEP!

And your quest will be—

BEEP! BEEP! BEEP! BEEP! BEEP!

Your quest will—

BEEP! BEEP! BEEP! BEEP! BEEP!

What in Jupiter's name is that awful beeping noise?

A red light illuminates on the dashboard. Your

fuel tank is almost empty and you might not have enough power to fly back to Miss Tentacle's School for Every Alien without filling-up.

"There is a space fuel station not far from here," notes BRIAN, with a press of her satnav button. "But it sells a different type of fuel to the one I use in this bus. There is a chance it will work well. But there is also a chance the new fuel will cause our bus to evaporate into a gazzilion tiny droplets of molten metal."

Blimey.

Well, this is quite a pickle. Will you risk filling-up with the new fuel, or see if you can make it back to school without it?

I'll carry on without filling up. Turn to page 34.

I'd like to go to the fuel station please. Turn to page 20.

As you steer your bus towards the giant star-cluster, a rocky planet appears in the distance. It's orbiting a tiny sun and a pale blue moon hangs in the hazy sky.

You drive closer. Could this be the planet you're looking for? There's definitely life here, although most of the buildings look really old-fashioned. There are neon signs in the windows and the sound of rock 'n' roll music is blasting out of their doors.

You see a row of spaceships next to a sign saying THE BLUE MOON DONUT CAFE and realise you've landed in the drive-through of an intergalactic diner.

Awesome!

There's a serving hatch to your right, so you open a window and lean out. A human-like alien with slicked-back hair and an upturned collar picks up a microphone, clears his throat and sings, "Welcome to the Blue Moon Donut Café. What can I get cha, uh huh huh?"

BRIAN's head appears over your left shoulder.

"Young humanoid," she says, "I do not think we should stop for donuts – we have not even located our first bus-stop yet."

She's right.

95

You know she's right.

But…*space-donuts?* They sound delicious!

Do you want to order some?

Yes, please – there's always time for donuts! Turn to page 84.

No, thank you – I'll ask the alien if we're on the right planet and get on with my quest. Turn to page 73.

A giant space-eel is scarier than a maths teacher with an algebra test, but bravely you face the beast and slowly press the accelerator.

The eel sees you. Its eyes narrow. It licks its gelatinous lips as a wicked smile creeps over its face. A bus full of children is like a tasty tin of baked beans to a giant space-eel and he wants you all in his belly.

Nom, nom, nom!

The monster opens its huge jaws and a bus-rattling roar blasts out of its mouth.

GRAAAAAAW!

As its teeth snap closed, you swerve left, whizz past its head and enter the planet's atmosphere. You should be safe in here – the eel can't leave the realms of its outer-space home.

But suddenly, the terrible beast whips out a tongue the size of Italy and wraps it around your bus like a frog catching a fly. A gloop of space-eel spit seeps in through an open window as you're pulled away from the planet and into the eel's mouth. It drips onto your lap like an unset jelly and then…

GULP!

The world goes dark.

Luckily, your bus is too crunchy for the space-eel to chew, so it swallows you whole and no-one gets hurt. You'll pass through the creature's digestive system in two to three days, along with everything else it has eaten today, by which time the children's parents will be sick with worry.

Try taking the huge fish by surprise on your next attempt, StoryQuester, and you'll soon be on your way to Aquatron.

Go back to the start of the book to try again, or turn to page 69 to make a different choice.

A giant space-eel is scarier than a maths teacher with an algebra test, but bravely you turn to the beast and slowly press the accelerator.

The eel sees you. Its eyes narrow. It licks its gelatinous lips as a wicked smile creeps over its face. A bus full of children is like a tasty tin of baked beans to a giant space-eel and he wants you all in his belly.

Nom, nom, nom!

The monster opens its huge jaws and a bus-rattling roar blasts out of its mouth.

GRAAAAAAW!

As its teeth snap closed, you swerve left, whizz past its head and enter the planet's atmosphere. You should be safe here – the eel can't leave the realms of its outer-space home.

But suddenly, the terrible beast whips out a tongue the size of Italy and wraps it around your bus like a frog catching a fly. A gloop of space-eel spit seeps in through an open window as you're pulled away from the planet and into the eel's mouth. It drips onto your lap like an unset jelly and then…

GULP!

The world goes dark.

Luckily, your bus is too crunchy for the space-eel to chew, so it swallows you whole and no-one gets hurt. You'll pass through the creature's digestive system in two to three days, along with everything else it has eaten today, by which time the children's parents will be sick with worry.

Try taking the huge fish by surprise on your next attempt, StoryQuester, and you'll soon be on your way to Aquatron.

Go back to the start of the book to try again, or turn to page 19 to make a different choice.

You decide to talk nicely to the toll collector and explain what happened.

"Hello," you say. "Erm, how are you?"

The alien smiles.

Actually, it could be a snarl.

Whatever it is, it looks like it hurts.

"Nrgh," growls the toll collector.

"I, erm, really like your clothes," you go on. "They're very—"

But then you realise she's a talking potato and she's not wearing any clothes. Awkward.

The toll collector pushes her hand closer towards you.

"You gotta pay," she says, "so gimme your money or *CLEAR OFF!*"

The force of her voice ruffles your hair and a drop of alien spit lands on your face.

"The thing is," you say, wiping it off with the back of your hand, "I'm on a quest to save these children, but I don't have any money. Please can you press the button and let me through without paying? Just this once?"

The toll collector curls her rubbery lips up under her nose and looks carefully into your eyes. Then she

shoves the forcefield button into her mouth and crunches it up like a boiled sweet.

CHOMP! CHOMP! CHOMP!

You take that as a 'no.'

The forcefield won't be opening any time soon, not now the button is inside the toll collector's belly, so you can't get to Sweatiolis to return the second group of children. Never mind, StoryQuester – why not go back and see if the toll collector would like a nice sandwich instead?

Go back to the start of the book to try again, or turn to page 29 to make a different choice.

When you open the window, a terrible stink fills the bus. It smells worse than a cabbage-eating skunk in a sewer.

"Phooey!" you cry, pinching your nose. "What's that horrible smell?"

"I believe the pong you're referring to comes from the fifteen moons of Sweatiolis," says BRIAN. "They are made out of cheese and are well-known for their astronomical whiff."

The stinky air makes your head dizzy and your vision blurred. You can't see to drive, so BRIAN presses the hologramophone button and the headmistress appears in the aisle of the bus, snoring like an elephant with a trumpet stuck up its nostril.

"ZZZZZZ! ZZZZZZ! ZZZZ- Oh, erm, hello," she splutters. "I was just resting my eyes." She wasn't. She was snoring like an elephant. "How can I help you?"

"Miss Tentacle, I am afraid the young humanoid has opened a window near the fifteen moons of Sweatiolis," explains BRIAN, "and the terrible whiff of cheese is overpowering their senses."

"That's awful news," says Miss Tentacle. "We must take the human back to an Earthean doctor as soon as possible. Wait there, BRIAN – I'll send someone out to fetch you."

A tow-ship arrives. It pulls you back to your home planet, where the doctor says you'll be fine but the smell lingers on you for weeks and everyone at school thinks you stepped in something a dog did.

Go back to the start of the book to try again, or turn to page 71 to make a different choice.

You decide to talk nicely to the toll collector and explain what happened.

"Hello," you say. "Erm, how are you?"

The alien smiles.

Actually, it could be a snarl.

Whatever it is, it looks like it hurts.

"Nrgh," growls the toll collector.

"I, erm, really like your clothes," you go on. "They're very—"

But then you realise she's a talking potato and she's not wearing any clothes. Awkward.

The toll collector pushes her hand closer towards you.

"You gotta pay," she says, "so gimme your money or *CLEAR OFF!*"

The force of her voice ruffles your hair and a drop of alien spit lands on your face.

"The thing is," you say, wiping it off with the back of your hand, "I'm on a quest to save these children, but I don't have any money. Please can you press the button and let me through without paying? Just this once?"

The toll collector curls her rubbery lips up under her nose and looks carefully into your eyes. Then she

shoves the forcefield button into her mouth and crunches it up like a boiled sweet.

CHOMP! CHOMP! CHOMP!

You take that as a 'no.'

The forcefield won't be opening any time soon, not now the button is inside the toll collector's belly, so you can't get to Sweatiolis to return the second group of children. Never mind, StoryQuester – why not go back and see if the toll collector would like a sandwich instead?

Go back to the start of the book to try again, or turn to page 55 to make a different choice.

Have you tried our new festive StoryQuest adventure? Deliver Santa's presents and save Christmas to complete your quest!

THE STOCKING FILLER

CHOOSE THE PAGE - UNLOCK THE ADVENTURE

A STORYQUEST BOOK BY
BECCI MURRAY

Available now in paperback or eBook.

Will you climb mountains and cross deserts to save the Sheriff's horse? Find out in this new Wild West adventure from StoryQuest.

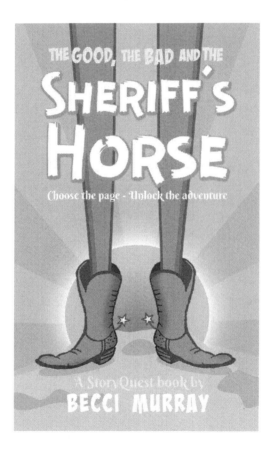

Available now in paperback or eBook.

Laugh along with Billy, as he boosts his brain to the size of Venus in this hilariously gruesome chapter book also by Becci Murray.

Or try these very serious poems about really important stuff (like sausages, yaks and toenails) in this illustrated collection of rhyming silliness.

Becci Murray is a British author from Gloucestershire. She used to run a children's entertainment company, where she earnt a living playing musical bumps and doing the Hokey Cokey (true story). Her favourite books are by Roald Dahl and she has a life-size BFG sticker on her bedroom wall (well, almost life-size).

You can learn more about Becci or send her a message by visiting the Llama House Children's Books website – she would love to hear from you!

www.llamahousebooks.com

Made in the USA
Columbia, SC
25 October 2020

23459122R00063